WHEN
It Starts
to SNOW

by
Phillis Gershator

Illustrated by
Martin Matje

SQUARE
FISH

Henry Holt and Company

New York

SQUARE
FISH

An imprint of Macmillan Publishing Group, LLC

Library of Congress Cataloging-in-Publication Data
Gershator, Phillis.
When it starts to snow / by Phillis Gershator ; illustrated by Martin Matje.
Summary: Various animals tell what they do and where they go when it starts to snow.
ISBN 978-0-8050-6765-1
[1. Snow–Fiction. 2. Animals–Fiction. 3. Stories in rhyme.] I. Matje, Martin, ill. II. Title.
PZ8.3.G3235Wh 1998   ffEtt–dc21   97-40698

Originally published in the United States by Henry Holt and Company
First Square Fish Edition: June 2012
Square Fish logo designed by Filomena Tuosto
Typography by Martha Rago
The artist used gouache and colored pencils on cardboard
to create the illustrations for this book.
mackids.com

21   23   25   27   29   30   28   26   24   22

To Holly, Megan,
David, and Christy
—P.G.

For Théophile
—M.M.

W hat if it starts to snow?
What do you do?
Where do you go?

"I creep into the house,"
says the mouse.
Cold winds blow
when it starts to snow.

"I sit by the window,"
says the cat.
Big eyes glow
when it starts to snow.

"I keep watch,"
says the shiny black crow.

when it starts to sno

"I look for seeds,"
says the sparrow.
Peck, peck, peck
when it starts to snow.

What if it starts to snow?
What do you do?
Where do you go?

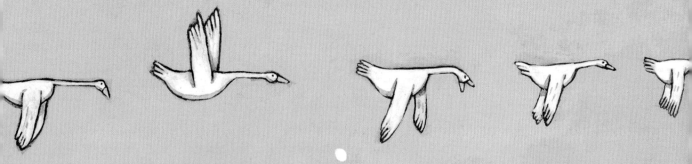

"We fly south," say the geese,
"all in a row."

HONK

HONK

HONK

when it starts to snow.

"I build a lodge," says the beaver.
"The work is slow."
Chop, chop, chop
when it starts to snow.

"The water is chilly," says the fish.
"It's best to lie low."
Swish, shhh, shhh
when it starts to snow.

"I go in the barn," says the pig,
"if it's too cold to hoe."

oink
oink
oink

when it starts to snow.

"I wait for the farmer,"
says the cow.
"He's coming, I know."
Moo, moo, moo
when it starts to snow.

What if it starts to snow?
What do you do?
Where do you go?

"I hide my eggs," says the hen,
"so the chicks can grow."
Cluck, cluck, cluck
when it starts to snow.

"I fly high up," says the rooster.
"Listen to me crow."
Cock-a-doodle-doo
when it starts to snow.

"I stay here," says the worm.
"It's warm down below."
Wiggle, dig, dig
when it starts to snow.

What if it starts to snow?
What do you do?
Where do you go?

"I wear a new coat," says the stoat,
"a king from head to toe."
White winter fur
when it starts to snow.

"I follow the turtle," says the frog.
"Down into the mud I go."
Peep, peep, peep
when it starts to snow.

"I look for a place," says the deer,
"where the moss and grasses grow."
Leap, leap, run
when it starts to snow.

"I dive down the hill," says the otter.
"I go with the flow."
Slip, slip, slide
when it starts to snow.

"Look," says the black bear,
"The snow is deep.
Hurry, scurry!
Time to sleep."

Bat in a cave.
Snake in a rock pile.
Raccoon in a log.
Squirrel in a hollow.

Mole in a tunnel.
Rabbit in a hole.
Wolf in a den.
Chipmunk in a burrow.

Snow on the roof.
Snow on the ground.
Brand-new snow

coming down,

coming down.

I can't sleep
when the snow wants to play.

Three cheers for snow!